Slag

Slag

Mansel Robinson

THISTLEDOWN PRESS LTD.

Canadian Cataloguing in Publication Data
Robinson, Mansel, 1955 –
SLAG
(New leaf editions)
ISBN 1-895449-73-1
I. Title. II. Series.
PS8585.035168S44 1997 C813'.54 C97-920165-9
PR9199.3.R5347S44 1997

Book design by A.M. Forrie
Set in 10 pt. New Baskerville
by Thistledown Press Ltd.

Printed and bound in Canada by
Veilleux Impression à Demande
Boucherville, Quebec

Thistledown Press Ltd.
633 Main Street
Saskatoon, Saskatchewan
S7H 0J8

The Canada Council for the Arts since 1957 | Le Conseil des Arts du Canada depuis 1957

We acknowledge the support of the Canada Council for the Arts for our publishing program. Thistledown Press also gratefully acknowledges the continued support of the Saskatchewan Arts Board.

ACKNOWLEDGEMENTS

The author gratefully acknowledges the financial assistance of the Saskatchewan Arts Board.

"Bullseye", originally titled "Hockey Nights In Canada", was published in *Takes*, (Thisledown Press, 1996).

"Sam Jr." aired on CBC Saskatchewan's *Gallery* and *The Arts Wrap* as "Ghost Trains: A Poem for Voice and Slide Guitar". Performed by Billy Morton; original music written and performed by Brent Nielsen; directed by Kelly-Jo Burke.

Thanks to Gary Geddes and Robert Allen, who read some of this work in an earlier form; to Rod MacIntyre for working on this version; and to my parents, Richard Rioux, Bill Cormier and dozens of friends and family at dozens of kitchen tables.

Thanks, as ever, to Ellen.

for Lionel, Whitney and Little Mac.

She says:

Your father is a brakeman awash on the mainline
he ships out on paper trains and fast freight
he rolls to the edge where the world begins
where teasing cities glisten.
Your mother walks the widow's walk till he lands home
plunder in hand and yarns to spice your soup.

The Canadian like a pocket liner steams over your horizon.
Port holes snap-shot past (exotic postcards)
lives in transit from edge to edge:
shy eyes turn
a hand raised to touch a cheek
the shake of her head.
The who what why who knows.
The secrets of sailors.

Pirates too. A hobo gritty with distance
whole continents under his nails.
He knocks on your back door, stacks firewood for bread
for a swallow of draft, like doubloons, gold.
Then gone again, four boxcars ahead of the cops
no port in mind
wheels under his feet on an inland sea.

At five and ten you dream this dream:
you wave from the shore, this black spruce shore.
You wave and wait. They sail.
They sail.

Joey says:

Wasn't money drove Sammy to the rails
not the promise finally of steady work and pay.
Depression hit his family hard
four dark winters of Relief
Christmas turkey from the church
his old man proud but broke then finally broken.
But wasn't money sent Sammy to the road at sixteen years.
Wasn't money it was talk:

> sunrise on the mainline
> steam and speed, muscle and machines
> small men who flower into heroes
> in the wreckage in the dark.

Romance clean and simple.

Wasn't words sent Sammy to the war
Democracy Freedom Hitler
God or Country
none of that.
Deadheadin *The Dominion* one night
five coaches full of WACS
a sweet smellin train
red heads and blue eyes and legs wherever he looked.
So Sammy joins up next month

no doubt dreamin skirt
the torpedoes hittin just offa Newphie
maybe still dreamin skirt
when they pluck him from the water

and dyin in a hospital train in Sudbury Yard
still railroadin
still romantic as hell.

Teddy says:

Communist. Biologist. Evangelist. I'll talk with anybody. I don't care. Sometimes it's an education. This is a good diner for talk, no TV and the food's pretty cheap. I work around here quite a bit, freelance you might say, wheels on my toolbox. And a lot of people end up talking to me. The last one to come around was some girl. I kept calling her girl even though it made her grind her teeth. I kept calling her girl *because* it made her grind her teeth. But she didn't call me on it, she was working on some theory and didn't want to piss me off. I wish she would have called me on the girl thing, I would have stopped. I was just trying to make a point. But she wasn't paying attention. Sometimes I wonder if that's what people with theories are, people who've stopped paying attention.

She bought me a coffee the way these people always do, buy your story for one spinning dollar. "Sociology," she said. "Global economy." "Dislocation of the workforce." "Migrant labour." She wanted to know how I was making out. I told her it wasn't that simple, I didn't feel like a passenger, but maybe she'd already stopped listening by then.

I told her I never learned much in school. The only important thing that happened to me in grade one was was seeing up Miss Gratten's dress. She wore pink panties and nothing she was teaching mattered much after that.

Arithmetic was like trying to turn a handful of air into a snowball, after ten minutes the timestables turned to smoke and I fell asleep. I could spell any word that came out of a mouth but the teachers never cared about those words. They only understood a word if it came out of a book. I might have liked books too but I never met anybody in one that I'd ever met in person so I gave up on reading. I could read a chimney though. Maybe they should teach that in school — reading chimneys.

I told her how some nights the smoke rises straight to the stars, not a curl or a loop, straight to the stars. I'd stand at my window, looking at the house across the street, thinking about a coal furnace chugging alone in a dark basement. I'd stand there watching the smoke until my feet got cold on the linoleum floor.

But this particular night the smoke was hanging loose from the chimney, twisting across the roof. It was the sign I was looking for — it was gonna snow. So I had work in the morning cleaning switches for the CPR, dollar forty an hour on the weekends. By 14, I still hadn't learned a thing in school but I could read that chimney. I climbed back into bed.

My mother wakes me up early.

"It's snowing hard," she says. She waits. "Steak's on." She waits. "I'll call you again in five minutes."

We were still on pretty good terms then. In a few years she'd be barging into my room complaining it smelled like a beer parlour, somehow making beer parlour sound like funeral parlour. "If you think you can drink like a man you can get up and work like a man." She didn't have a sense of humour about some things. One time I had a T-shirt made up — "Work — the curse of the drinking class". First time she saw it she looked at me with three eyes blazing. I guess maybe booze was sloshing around in her family pretty good but we never heard about her family at all.

I came downstairs for breakfast.

Breakfast in a warm kitchen when it's still dark outside is still the best meal of the day. Lunch is going to be piss-warm tea and a cold sandwich and by supper time some foreman'll have tracked his boots up and down your spine. So breakfast at home is like going to church. Work's OK — It's the people you gotta watch.

"Dad out on the road?"
"Called for the snowplow at three."

There's a story went around about this brakeman and his wife. She used to laugh at him, said the reason he had such a big gut was that he never did anything on the trains, just sat on his fat ass watching the trees go by. He took it for a few years. One night at three a.m. he parks a kitchen chair in front of the window, wakes her up and ties her into the chair. "Ok," he says. "You stare out this window for 6 hours, you stay awake, you keep your eyes open, you don't miss a thing. Then you come talk to me about my job." Nobody knows what anybody else does for a living. You see a man leaning on his shovel and you call him lazy, you say something about government jobs. You don't go check to see how deep the hole is. But my mother understood railroading and she'd always pack the old man's grip in the middle of the night.

I ate my breakfast. Toast and fried baloney. *Sirloin de Caboose,* we called it. My mother didn't laugh about booze but she didn't mind bad jokes about her cooking. Good thing.

Outside it was still kinda dark, snow coming down in flakes as big as silver dollars. The grader hadn't been down our street yet and only Mr. Lane was out cleaning his path. Saturday mornings the town kicked over slow and mornings like this the snow wrapped a baffle around the sound. It looked good — a black dog down the street and Mr. Lane red-faced in his yard.

The section shack smelled like wet fur from the steam heat. The foreman was doing his paperwork. Pretty soon the guys were coming in. There were jokes about hangovers and I heard my sister's name. Eddy threw up out behind the shack, promising to the Virgin Mary he was done with lemon gin. Eight o'clock we grab our brooms and shovels and head into the Yard.

Cleaning switches was the first job I had that gave something back. Forget delivering newspapers or pumping gas. But you come to a switch that's jammed up with snow and ice and it's just a broken tool, junk. But you work at it, clean the points out, the rods, you work at it until it's a machine again and running smooth, you can throw that switch easy as flipping an egg. And when you head over to the next jammed up switch you can turn around and see what you've done: clean as a gun barrel, cared for, working.

My toes freeze up by nine o'clock. We work till noon.

Back in the shack I eat my baloney sandwich, thaw out my feet. Eddy's curled up in a pile of parkas. All the Friday night lies start to grow legs and walk around on their own. I hear my sister's name again. I go outside.

The Canadian's sitting on the main line. It's about eight hours late, probably frozen steam lines from the long pull across the prairies. I'd only ever seen this train at night, I'd never seen it sitting in the daylight, all that glass and stainless steel and shining like a newborn thing. My parka stinks with creosote and my fingernails are blue. I'm staring out from under my hood into the windows of the club car. There's a woman drinking from a white mug and looking down at the table in front of her, probably reading. Once, she looks out the window, looks down the station platform, past the baggage carts and the water tower. She goes back to her book. I'm thinking there's nobody in this town ever looked like her.

At another window there's a guy drinking beer. He looks out at the station buildings, run-down and ugly. He waves for another beer. He looks lonely. But I don't feel sorry for him.

Two black porters are hanging out of an open door. One of them points up to mainstreet and they grin.

The engineer gives two quick tugs on the whistle and *The Canadian* starts to move. The wheels turn slowly, I can hear frozen metal and see clouds of steam rolling up from under the coaches. The snow is coming down harder now, my parka turning white. I don't go back inside the shack until the train is long past the mile-board. I'm thinking about nothing but the laughing black porters and the man drinking a beer and a beautiful woman reading a book, miles away.

I don't need ten buck words to talk about it. If I'd eaten two baloney sandwiches for lunch one particular day I might be somebody else. No big deal. Most things aren't. You snag a fish hook in your finger and the next thing you know you're upside down in the rapids with the tump-line twisted around your ankles. You drown from a fish hook in your finger. Accidents spin our world and ten buck words don't change that. When the theory of relativity fell out of the sky my grandmother still had to get up next morning to milk the cows.

This coffee here, gone cold. No steam at all. It was no big deal. Only the weather. On a colder kind of night that smoke would have gone straight to the stars.

Great Uncle Ben says:

We spot my caboose on the back track
open Chapleau's only rolling casino
no wheels or craps
no high rollin chicanery
straight poker, shut your mouth and deal
hands where we can see em.

Three weeks around the clock the coal-oil burns
half a thousand hours of check and call
paychecks on the blanket
good folding money changing pockets.

Brakemen and engineers sit in between trips between
the chores at home between the wife's contractions
whisky from a mug, sandwiches trotted by the box
from the Boston Café.

The class system at work (working overtime)
running trades only, a sectionman or car-knocker
allowed to sit in but only if he's a damn good man
(a pair of mediocre brakemen beats three section foremen.)

And like I said three weeks in 1910 the coal-oil burns.
Yardmaster at last bangs in the door
"Just what the *hell* is going on?"
"Redistribution of wealth" I says.
And scoop the pot.

The Old Man says:

Slippery stalls her going up the grade at O'Brien
has to double over the hill, pulls in three hours late.
The Brass scream for brownie points.

Slippery fidgets on The Carpet (he's been there before)
squints the bosses up and down
rifles through his deck of alibis:

poor coal — therefore no steam
green fireman — consequently no fire
swarms of grasshoppers — resulting in greasy rail —
ipso facto, no traction.

But he lays "over-tonnage" on the table —
trump.

Well sir
I pull her out at ten aught five
51 cars and we're makin fine time
coal that'd do the Devil proud
the steel as dry as a Methodist wake.
The grade at Bolkow? We fly over it like we're haulin
(he hitches up his overalls)
like we're haulin air, light as bird song.
By the time we come to the controlling grade
(O'Brien you know) it's 21 hundred hours, evening gentlemen,
and the cargo, need I remind you we we're haulin canaries?
and the cargo, gentlemen, the little beggars go to roost.
I can feel the drivers start to slip
(he paws with his hands) slipping as the birds bed down

51 cars of bird-song now 51 cars of dead damn weight.
Gentlemen. Sudden and unequivocal over-tonnage.
Not a blessed thing I could do.

The Brass slap 20 brownies on his record
but Slippery is off to the Legion Hall
a smirk behind his moustache
his tail in the air
and a new line of bull for the boys.

Sammy says:

20 cents between us, a cord of wood
split and stacked behind the house
our palms hot from the axe and maul
big shots laughing in the Boston Café.

My cousin Joey starts in with "kitty fried rice"
we giggle and slurp our ginger beer
won ton pussy cat
curried bat's eyes
sucker lip suey.

Hong Kong Fong fills a coffee mug
wipes a table down, barely looks our way
Joey hiccups for egg foo opium
waves like a big shot for the bill.

It looks like a joke but
Hong Kong Fong doesn't smile
so we don't say a thing
leave the whole two dimes where they sit

walk home not laughing
not knowing what he means
knowing he means what he means:

2 ginger beers	10 cents
2 head tax	1000 dollars
total	1000 dollars, ten cents.

Bullseye says:

I had a twin brother for a while. He's gone now. He became somebody he wasn't supposed to be. We were born with the same face then he took that face and put it where it didn't belong.

We grew up in a small town that only had one band. They used to play at the Legion Hall about once a month. They learned a new song every couple of years. They called themselves *The Rhythm Renegades.* We called them *The Frozen Five.* I guess making music is hard. I don't know. I never tried. My brother never did either. He only ever tried one thing. But in that one thing he was a magician. He'd set himself up for a rebound like he could read the future. He could stick handle so slick you never saw the puck 'til the red light blinked. No other word for it. Magician.

His name was Corky. Pretty good name I guess. It's got a bit of something to it, and it coulda been famous, like Boom Boom or Toe. One time when we were about six we were playing hockey in the street. Corky lifted a slap shot up about three feet that caught me right in the head. It left a perfect half-circle scar right over the eyebrows. Next year when we joined minor hockey they stuck me in nets. They called me Bulls-eye. That's the name I go by even now. Bulls-eye. I don't know what name Corky goes by these days. Maybe he gave that up too. I don't know.

I just wanted to skate. That's what I loved. One strange winter it hardly snowed at all. The wind kept the river swept clean for maybe a month. I'd skate for a mile or so, east and west. I knew the river better that winter than the ducks knew it in the summer. But I joined hockey and the coach went and stuck me in nets — he put me in the cage. I didn't really love the game, didn't really love it at all. Only wanted to skate. To me, that was like walking on water. Like racing against a white-tailed deer. Like dancing. But goalies don't dance. They wait. They called me Bulls-eye for a reason.

Twins, they said. But Corky had the magic wrists and I barely learned to juggle. I was OK as a goalie, but nothing even close to special. I took my twenty turns around the rink during warm-up then took my place at the end of the bench.

I got my skating done in other ways. Friday nights I'd go to the rink, the same ten scratchy records going round and round like the skaters. Then after hockey was finished for me I got a job at the rink. A few guys were paid to clean the ice between periods and after the games. Laced up our skates and pushed the snow off the ice with shovels. We skated round and round with our shovels like little machines. They have real machines now. Zambonis. They called us rink rats.

I played even after I was too old for minor hockey. Something to do. Monday nights a few of us would rent the rink — we got it cheap because I worked there. We had a jug of vodka and orange juice in the penalty box. You shoulda seen the line-up of guys wanting to get a penalty. My brother was playing Junior by this time but he used to drop by once in a while to check us out. He called us *The Monday Night Misfits.*

You know what I wanted? I wanted to dance on the ice. I wanted to be a figure skater. But you didn't say that too loud around here. Those boys who wore the figure skates were accidently on purpose made to feel unwelcome — they kinda drifted out of town one by one. I wanted to dance. And I never did. I loved to watch the figure skaters though. Dancing on water.

Corky. He had a one-way ticket out of town — one-way to the top. Money. Girlfriends. Whatever he wanted. He loved the game. He gave it up when he was nineteen. I don't know why. He just stopped. Cold. He had all that magic and he laughed at it. The son of a gun did nothing but watch it disappear.

Every once in a while somebody asks me why I never moved from here, never left home. I find that a funny question somehow. I would never ask somebody, *Why do you believe in God?* You either do or you don't. I don't see what there is to mess with. But sometimes when somebody asks me I give them an answer anyways. I tell them this: one time I went to Hearst with the team. I was doing my job — bench warming, riding the pine. A back-up in case the starting goalie skated off the face of the earth.

We stayed in a hotel and we all stayed up late, talking about the sex we were going to have some day and having water fights in the meantime. The coach finally got everybody settled down and the hotel was quiet. It was about three in the morning. I wasn't sleepy so I was standing looking out the window. I saw a woman come walking down the street by herself. She was right in front of my window when a guy on an old skidoo stopped beside her. They talked for a bit. I thought maybe they were friends. Then he grabbed her and threw her on the seat of the skidoo. Then he sat on her and drove down the street. Right past the police station. She was screaming. And then it was quiet again.

Sometimes I tell people that's why I never left this town. Sometimes they understand.

I don't know why Corky threw his magic away. Maybe it came too easy for him.

Or maybe it wasn't even me who saw that woman and the skidoo. Maybe it was him standing at the window, hearing her scream, unable to move.

Johhny Hill says:

Dougie D's been drinkin.
Bottle after bottle of creme de menthe his eyes
not red but green.

The call boy's on the phone: you're called for 901.
Can't work tonight, better book me off.
Boss says can't book you off.
OK, so book me sick.
Can't book you sick, boss says.

Then Jesus Christ book me
dead.

Uncle Gilles says:

East of Nemegos, Janacek sings railroad aesthetics
the long steel winches past, rollers humming chorus.

This quarter mile rail, look, the whole world's changin.
The rhythm of the trains is steel on steel, the clickety clack
the clickety clack is wheel smackin rail joint every 32 feet.
What kind of song you get from quarter mile steel?

Quiet as a dog's tail
a long rail wags off the last roller
answers Janacek up the inside of his thigh
flap-jacks him ten feet high.

He lands arse over tea kettle
comes up spitting slag and teeth still
talking through his butt
"Compo, goin on compensation now . . . "

And then he dips his fingers
in the red muck behind his fly
barks to a blue moon
and tips towards darkness.

Uncle Slide says:

You wanna know messy?
Put a stock-train in the bush.

We jumped track a few years back near mileage 61
nothin but guts for 200 yards.
Hills of baloney stinkin in the heat
pigs in the swamp pigs in the trees
chubby old porkers ke-bobbed in the poplars.
Cows like they'd been browsin on track torpedoes.
But that's the easy part, bulldoze em under
the Company calls insurance.

But you ever seen pigs runnin loose in the bush
cows crazy with fear?
(Don't blame em at all, I bellied a Lanc in '44
'd rather do that than jump track doin fifty.)
So there we are pigs screamin in the night
the Company paying trackmen to chase ham on the hoof.
Black fly season too.
Maybe the cows weren't so bad, lazy I guess
but pigs are fast and a few got away.

About two years back
they fired a signal maintainer worked outta here.
Came back to the station one day bawlin about pigs —
yappin and snappin he says, man-eaters,
eyes as ugly as the muzzle of a three oh three
wouldn't let him off the motor car.
Roadmaster had him fired for DT's on the job.

But whaddya know, last year we lost that roadmaster.
Right at mile board 61.
Whatever got him ate his packsack and his new boots too.

Corky says:

We're running for home after track patrol
black spruce getting blacker the day sliding away.
Eddy checks his watch a third time
and slaps the throttle back.

No need to ask. Two men dead at Loon last Tuesday
read us the rule book:
motorcars don't bluff a freight.

We sit at the take-off reach for cigarettes
matches flame and snuff in the wind.
Eddy swears at dispatchers blue fingernails at god
above the snow clouds. Eddy speaks three languages
all of them foul. I fantasize dry socks
pea soup and whisky.

There he is says Eddy at the whistle, bout fuckin time.
I cross the track to inspect from the other side.
The roll and rumble works up the right of way
the headlamp teasing with warmth.
The engineer waves from the warm living room of her cab
an easy grin as she goes by.
I watch for bad axles and dragging gear.
When the caboose clanks pass we're on our way.

Whaddya think Eddy, sight for sore eyes eh?
Christ, he says, dumping the car on the track
sixty grand a year. When women cut into the railroad pie
they didn't help themselves to the crust
now did they?

(But late last week his daughter hires on
for trial trips.)

Liz says:

He called for help on the radio. They thought he was joking but his conductor found him pinched between two boxcars, alive and quiet, cinched tight at the waist by the couplers. Veins blue and thick on his neck. Legs dead and dangling. Waiting. A kind of saw-the-man-in-two mad magic trick you never try at home. The doctor was called and they talked it over. He could wait, a day, two, till his broken insides turned slow to poison. Or they could pull the cars apart and that would be that. Both ways the end was the same. They talked it over, and finally they called me down to say good-bye. The pin was pulled, the boxcars moved.

Only he was cut and crushed no doubt about that, but still of a piece. (More or less.) So they ladled him up to the hospital for five dull months in bed.

People see him on the street these days, walking slow, and people say what a shame. I like to look on the bright side — at least he's quit screwing around.

Floyd says:

I am an intelligent worm.
I crawl into the earth. I eat rock. I crawl back to the surface. I excrete gold.
Crawl into the earth. Eat rock. Crawl to the sunlight. Excrete gold.
Excrete cobalt. Excrete bauxite. Nickle. Uranium. Copper.
Intelligent worms crawl into the earth eat rock shit money and wait.
Wait for the lungs to turn brown. Or black. Till they glow in the dark.
Wait for the roof to cave in.
Wait for the draegermen scratching through a million tons of the Canadian Shield.
I am an intelligent worm.

I'm two miles underground. Two miles underground doing my job.
Business as usual.
Then it all blows up in my face.
I don't remember the explosion.
Maybe it was something like a Sylvester Stallone movie. Loud. Expensive. Stupid.
I don't remember waking up.
I remember the pain.

Day one, I'm singing songs. Folk songs.

I love to go swimmin
with bowlegged women
and swim between their knees.

Rock n roll songs. The Ramones: "I Wanna Be Sedated".
Day two I'm remembering old jokes.
Two guys in a bar. They get talking about Northern Ontario. One guy sneers. Timmins, he says. Only thing ever came out of Timmins was whores and hockey players.
Other fella says — my wife's from Timmins.
First fella says — Really? What team does she play for?

I'm thinking about my coke habit. I'm thinking: there's gotta be a way to get that much pharmaceutical intake onto my drug plan.

I'm thinking about stories I heard at home. My uncle Dan crying about the dying of the railroads.
Crazy Uncle Dan says:
I go into a pawn shop. I been there before. Just a pawnshop. But today. Today — behind the counter sits John A. MacDonald himself, pouch-eyed, whiskey breath. He nods toward a shelf of tools, bucksaws and augers. In the face of a hammer shocked smooth by a million nails I imagine a roofer on his knees Monday to payday, and in the handle polished by callous and sweat, I see his shingles shed rain.

John A. nods again, points to a bucket of metal shop tools, grinding discs and vise grips, a wire brush. Then I see the reason for his nod. I see that the last spike has been pawned. You know the spike I mean, "Stand Fast Craigellachie", the last stitch in the twin silver ribbons, the last inches anchored in the sea to shining sea. Does it glitter? No. As iron as any in the line, it glitters only in dreams, glitters in dreams especially.

I take the spike in my hand. It's pocked with the track hammer blows of Donald Smith and of the sectionmen who worked the line. I see rails crack from frost and over-tonnage, the spikes clawed out, the ties chopped in three by the tie-gang and burned on the slag. I see the steel-gang rolling through the canyon with quarter-mile rail and pneumatic machines. I hold this thing passed hand to hand, attic to attic, and finally abandoned here, rusted and for sale.

John A. coughs. I ask him: is it really the last spike? They shed dreams, he says; they shed dreams like snakes shed skin.

Mostly I'm trying not to think about my son.

Day three I'm making up my own mythololgy.
That cave in Spain.
Those crazy rocks: chandeliers of stalactites; candelabra stalagmites. Some wild sci-fi opera set.
And the drawings on the wall.
Cavemen stuck in the caves during the snows, sick of each other, sick of waiting, sick of thinking. So they draw these animals, buffalo and reindeer, to remind themselves of the world outside. It's not magic or religion. It's just a locket next to the heart of winter to remind them of the sun.

Day four I'm licking the walls.

Day five I drink my urine.
I puke.
Time passes.
I lick up the puke.
I get used to the taste of piss.

Day six I hallucinate.
Great whacking slabs of hallucinations.
Some woman, she's about three hundred pounds. Shaved head and rubber boots. No teeth. And we're doing it. In an upper berth on *The Canadian.* The train's rocking, she's on top, three hundred pounds of railroad jello. Then she starts to laugh. She laughs and laughs. What's so funny, I say. Your dick, she says. What's so funny

about my dick, I say. It tickles, she says. It tickles. My dick gets even smaller, gets littler and littler, she's laughing harder and harder. Then we're pulling into the station. There's a marching band. I get off the train. I'm wearing her rubber boots. My head is shaved. I got no teeth. And I got no dick. The conductor tries to bum a buck for coffee but I got no money. And when the train pulls out of the yard, that women is driving.

My withered dick. No hallucination.

Day seven I'm thinking about bones in the slag.
Almost everybody I know.
Blaine Alrich. Falls into a debarker, some mill near Kapuskasing.
Johnny Hill. Out on the mailine. Lousy track.
Larry Wallace. Out on the mainline. China White.
Kelly McWatch. Log truck hits his train near Cartier.
Aunt Bev. Black ice and a rock cut. That'll teach her to drive sober.
Jimmy Scott. Some greener kills em both scaling.
Doug McNab. Drunk on the job.
Gerry Koski. Heat stroke on the Gulf of Thailand. Hey Buddy! Wear a hat!
Tim Dube. His brother shoots him. Accident. We say.
Tommy Beulieu. No. He's in jail. Kills his wife's boyfriend.
Sam Mah. Falls out of his boat duck hunting. Goof.
Bob Wilson. Found dead in bed with the sheets full of porno. Guess which kind?
Sarah Thomson. Roof. Thought she had wings. Now she does.
Kenny Righetti. .22 long in the head. Took him two days to die.
I wouldn't use a .22 to kill myself.
12 gauge.
Brainpan stuccoed to the kitchen ceiling.
Gonna do a job, make sure you do it right.
Protestant work ethic.

I'm thinking: this town is cursed.
I'm thinking: No surprise.
We're on an Indian graveyard.

First shaft of the mine. Sunk her right through the bones.
Ribs in the slag.

Mostly I'm thinking about my son.
I'm thinking I wish he was in school somewhere, being a teacher a lawyer, an accountant. Something. Anything. Even a double-gut brakeman. Doing anything anywhere but down here.
I'm wondering if he made it out.
I'm praying.

Day eight, the kobalds are scratchin on the walls. Kobalds. Koblynau. Goblins in the mines. Dead miners who never died. Dead men breathing rock. A brush of stale air when they go past. Mucking shift after shift until the sun goes cold and then for one shift after that.
I figure I'm dying.
So I take my place on the kobald shift.
A Goblin.

I don't remember the draegermen digging me out.
I don't remember the hospital: Demerol. Actually — I do remember the Demerol.
I *like* Demerol.

I get out of the hosptial.
I drink.
I drink.
I drink more.

This is my chair. This is my table. There's something about this arrangement that comforts me, my back against the once-white wall. Two glasses in front of me like the levers on an old D-7. Left. Right. Straight ahead.
This place. Bush leaguers, mooches, cuckolds. Suits. Rednecks. Eunuchs. A flotilla of drinkers rise and fall with the tide.
Bald guy in the corner thinks he fought in Vietnam, calls himself No Slack, dreams of being a mercenary. Lives on Maalox n' Labatt's 50. And there's nothing shaking for him but his hands.

Alzheimers Allstars hooked to the sports channel like an iron lung. One of em last week hobbles out of the john with his pants to his knees and blood in his jockeys bawling how he thinks he's dying. But it's not the dying that spooks him — drowning by the ounce takes time.

Me I've taken my stand sitting down. Look behind me. Been here so long there's a template on the wall, head and shoulders in the tobacco yellowed paint. White shadow gonna be here until the sea level rises or they hose this place down. Whichever comes first.

One day my boy comes in. He sits across the table from me. Doesn't say a thing. Just sits and looks at me.
Half his face is gone, brains smeared down his cheek, one eye popped out, left arm ripped off at the elbow, ankles so crushed he's wearing both feet backwards. He just sits and looks at me.
Then he says: Daddy. You got business to take care of.
Fucking Hamlet, right? I mean, sort of.
Don't sweat it. I been to high school.
We just sit there looking at each other. Then he reaches in his pocket and takes out his ear. He drops it in my beer.

Then he starts to talk. To me. Which is unusual cause he never talks to me.

Johnny says — he says:
I don't know who, what, where, when or why. I don't remember the first time I saw a game or heard Danny Gallivan on the tube. I don't remember the first time I heard the slash of skates on the ice. But I wanted to play in the NHL before I could spell it. I wanted to be Dave Keon before I knew where Toronto was. I practiced my slapshot all summer in your basement, fuck the sun, and baseball was for sissies. I only felt alive when my feet were slowly freezing solid inside my skates. Schoolbooks were wasted wood, they shoulda made sticks instead. I was 18 before I knew that a Hespeler Mic-Mac was named after an Indian tribe.
There was only one good thing about summer. Late summer anyway. I'd go down to the rink and sneak in. There'd be a coupl'a

guys repairing the pipes for the ice. You could smell the ammonia. I'd sit in the cool wooden stands, look up and see bits of blue sky through the holes in the roof.

When it got colder, they'd haul the fire hoses out and start spraying. Rainbows from the spray. The pipes turn white with frost. After a while there's a thin cover of snow over the bed of sand under the pipes. And then the ice starts to form. The ice is black, like river ice. A few days later they'd start painting. They'd paint the whole sheet white. Then the red line. Blue lines. Face-off spots and circles. I'd go home and tape up a new stick with a new roll of black tape.

When it all started to come together for me it came together fast. I slipped through minor hockey like the smart kids skipped grades. I was playing with guys who looked like they shaved twice a day and I never got their jokes but I got the goals. I was embarrassed so I kept my underwear on in the dressing room, hairless and clueless. Like the first time I heard the word motherfucker. I wondered what in hell is going on in *that* family.

Junior B. Junior A. Farm team. Boom boom boom. Then the mid-season call up.

Do you remember the first time you ever made love? Do you remember saying to yourself, we're actually here, naked, together, thousands of hours thinking about it, but here we are, finally, me and her. It isn't a daydream or a movie. It's here on my fingertips, in my sweat.

Four games. Two hundred and forty minutes.

Then I took a hard check, stepped on a landmine at the blue line. Blew my knee into forty pieces.

I'd been dreaming for 19 years. Two hundred and forty minutes later . . .

I think everybody is born with one dream. Just one. The dream either comes true or it doesn't. But you only get one, no matter what. You don't get a chance to change it if what comes through is a big disappointment. You don't get a chance to change the dream even if you realize it'll never come true. After fifteen or twenty years you've got no time or energy or ablity to start

dreaming again.
I don't know if you've noticed this: sometimes if you pass by the washroom in the tavern, you can hear the water if the door swings open just as conversation lulls for a moment. I don't know if you've noticed, but if you're just drunk enough, not too straight not too sober, you can hear it. The flushing of the water sounds just like . . .
applause.

I didn't say anything. My usual style with him. He looked at me with his one good eye then he got up and left.

I just sat there looking at his ear in my glass. Sat there listening to the urinals run. They didn't sound like applause. More like a set of rapids you shouldn'ta run.

Two days later I check myself into spin-dry. Twenty eight days in detox on the taxpayer's tab, tracking bloody paw prints in and out of group therapy until all the fluid's gone.

My name is Floyd and I'm an alcoholic. Uh. Yeah, well. I guess I've always been a partyer. Since high school anyway. Un. Old Vienna. Started on Old Vienna. That's what my old man drank. Most of you guys must've known him. Railroader. Anyway. I liked the smell of beer on the old man on a hot day. I remember the taste of my first beer, the neighbour who gave it to me had magnificient tits. I remember a Sudbury drunk-tank, a sheet-iron mattress green as shit on a creme-de-menthe bender. And I remember coming to at three a.m. with my wife's hands around my throat.
Her subtle way of saying goodbye.
I'm not used to being out of work. I got my first job when I was thirteen, been broke ever since. Yeah, uh. So I'm pounding 'er back pretty good these days. Start on beer about noon then get to the serious stuff around happy hour.

My name is Floyd. I'm an alcoholic. I shoot junk. I read dirty magazines. Live with it.

No. Detox ain't for me.

But I still got business to fix so I make a call.
I'm saying, long distance to this friend I'm saying:
I got a dead son. Three dead men more. Four widows and five orphan rug-rats.
I'm saying:
Long distance I'm saying:
I'm a gimp.
I'm saying:
Violence and greed. Pay-offs and missing files.
I'm saying: human stupidity.
I'm saying:
You're a journalist. I got a story. You can write it. You gotta write it.
Long distance I'm saying: You're my friend. I need you.
I'm saying please.

I remember my friend when he was a size-four momma's boy. I remember him when he was skating on his ankles. I remember him in the highschool year book: "the perfect combination of brains and brawn".
Sometimes you see him on the 11 o'clock news, small town boy makes good, taking on the big shots.
One time he tells me:
You know why I despise politicians? They're partridges. They sit in a tree with no leaves, purring and whirring like a goddamn *folk* musician and they wonder why they end up in the goddamn frying pan. You know what you need to hunt partridge? Time and a serious lack of ambition. They think they're invisible. They strut through the airport with their bimbos and bum-boys, yakking off in the departure lounge, dropping Visa receipts like feathers. They sell their souls at eight o'clock on a Friday night in some chi-chi beanery to some third cousin fronting for the Mob. They leak to anyone with a notebook. And then they wonder why they end up on page one with the horse cops half way up their prostate.
Dumb.
Partridge dumb.

I need a guy who's pissed off. So I call him long distance.
Long distance he says:
Maybe.

So I wait.
And I live.
And life starts to pile up.

Yeah. How are you today? Look, uh. My compo cheque's late. Every time I phone I can't get through or I get put on hold and spend the afternoon listening to Elton John. It's not that I'm in love with compensation, I'd rather be working but I'm not working and I'm not about to be working and the cheques put growlies in my freezer. You know what I mean? So let's start again. My cheque's two weeks late. If you want to talk to my mortgage officer, lemme guess, he's your twin brother, you guys all sound the same. No no no. *Here*'s the deal. I got dinged on the job. I'm entitled to the money. I want the money. And I want it on time. If it weren't for us cripples, you wouldn't have a job. So why don't you get on it and get me some cash. I know you can track down that missing moolah, you got eight grand of taxpayer's money sitting on that desk in front of you, 486 Pentium chip 4-wheel drive dual exhaust racing stripes all-weather radials and intergalactic hoo-haw. So find out where my cheque is or I'll be sitting right here until you qualify for old age pension.

I see a doctor.

I'm not asking for a lecture so don't lecture me. I'm not scamming you for drugs, not double dipping prescriptions. I'm telling you what's going on. The crap you prescribe is absolute crap. What are you doing, giving me placebos, is this some kind of experiment, someone else getting the real goods, are you kidding me? Some useless freebies from the drug company you're passing off? Forget it. I got my own dope now, guy I know takes good care of me, it's clean, it does the job quick and easy, only problem is medicare doesn't cover it. I'm not gonna kill myself — unless I have to start hanging around the garbage cans at the hospital picking up used syringes. You hearing me? All I want is clean works and lots of them. I can't exactly start dating a nurse who'll help me out, can I? Ethics. Jesus Christ. Ethics?

I go to physio.

I'm gonna ask you a question. But you don't have to answer. You're helping me out and I like you and I don't want to piss you off. But I'm curious.
When you go home at night. To whatever kind of body you go home to. What do you see?
What do you *think about* about what you see?
I'm assuming your — lover — is a complete package: head, arms, legs, eyes, ears, etc. etc. But you been with us crips all week, not a complete package in the bunch, maybe make up one full-sized guy if you cannibalized our parts, but actually at the moment we're jury-rigged outta wheels and thingamajigs and pullies and plastic and zinc and ball bearings, transitors and computer chips, and all the miracles of the technological revoultion.
So you do 40, 50, 60 hours a week with us human, *ratios*, five parts flesh to three parts aluminum.
So I'm wondering. What's real to you? Two legs or one?
See. When I'm underground, I'm in a place no human being is supposed to be. When I blast out a stope and then I'm mucking out rock in a place no human being has ever *ever* been before, forget Star Trek, I'm inside solid rock where no living thing has ever breathed oxygen. And that's just — unreal. But after 20 years, the unreal becomes the real. And the real — the sun, the trees, the perch in the lake — that becomes the unreal. I'm talking about work here. What we do, defines the real. Everything else, becomes questionable.
So like I said. What's real? The cripple? Or the whole package?

Yeah. I'm seeing all kinds of people. Tits on a nun. So I'm sticking to veterinary science —
"coke is for horses, not for men,
doctor says'll kill me, but he don't say when."

But since the compo cheque is always late and always small. And since a career in the ballet is out of the question. I go looking for work.

You gotta give me this job. You gotta. You got the perfect candidate sitting right here in front of you. The ad you placed? Me. It's like my whole, biography, for god's sake, it's like I was reading my entire life's story when I read your ad. My history, my — dreams, my — the way I walk. OK. Not the way I walk, but you know what I mean? My *mother* doesn't know me any better, she couldn't describe me better than you did in that ad. The successful applicant would be: me. I know, I know. I'm tooting my own tin horn, right? I never do that. Really. I'm a humble kind of person. But when I read that ad, Jesus, I felt like Moses or something, the dark clouds opened up or whatever, and you're talking to *me.* Just me.

How many people in this town read that ad? Hundreds. Dozens. But it wasn't written for them. It was written for me. And I know it. And you know it.

It's like you and I knew each other in another life time. Like maybe we were separated at birth. Are you sure you're not adopted, we look a bit alike, it's the nose, our noses are a bit off centre, see? Barely noticeable. Cause if we were — siblings — if we were, wouldn't that be wild? Working together after all these years. You and me. Family.

Getting crazy out there eh? Line-up halfway down the stairs to apply for one little job. To apply to be trained for a job.

Remember the days you could quit a job, walk three blocks and pick up a better one? Want ads? Man, the papers had no room for news so many want ads. These days all the want ads are in the personals. White woman seeking black man. Short man seeking tall woman. Blind man seeking deaf man with seeing eye dog.

Everybody's looking.
But whaddya say? Something about salary expectations in the ad,

don't worry about it. I don't need that much, I can live on, not peanuts maybe, but I can live on, not much. Really. Hours too. I don't care. Days. Nights. Weekends, holidays, Christmas, what do I care about Christmas for, I got no kids. Not now, I mean. I never liked Christmas anyway, but now . . . Look. Sorry. You probably don't want to get into my personal stuff. It's just — I feel I know you cause you know me so well, my life story's in that one little ad. The perfect candidate.
Whaddya say?
You gonna give me this job?

Not a bad pitch eh?
But the job . . .

Uh. Hello. Mrs. Jones. Hi. Uh. Listen. Have you every had your chimney reamed out by a professional?
Whaddya mean, "vaguely pornographic"? I asked her if she wanted her chimney swept, isn't that what we're selling here?
So I'm having a bad morning.
So I'm having a bad *week.*
Buddy. I'm having a bad *life.*
What do you want from me? If I was good with people you think I'd spend the last 20 years a mile under the goddamn ground.
No no you got *me* wrong. I *love* this work. I wanna do this forever, the career of the millenium, career choice of millions of college grads from North Bay to Pickle Crow. Cutting edge, you know what I'm saying? To hell with blue collar the bush and the mines and the factory. Who needs that shit when you can sell somebody something he already has, will never use, doesn't want or that does not yet exist.
I tell ya. Coming here taught me one thing — a man does not pull his weight in this world unless he can work the telephone. All other workers are just parasites.
I am trying. It's just that it's gonna take me a while to learn how to suck butt professionaly. Cause that's what it is. Professional butt sucking. I watched you demonstrate, I seen you wiggle your head

so far up the customer's sphincter I thought we were gonna have to tie a safety line to your ankle so we didn't lose ya up his ass.

I'm getting desperate.
I see a preacher.

I'm gonna be honest with you, Rev. This isn't my idea. My mother phoned. She thinks, I need help: the big guns, smart bombs, the H-bomb. She thinks I need, God. So I'm making her happy. OK? When she calls next week to ask me if I've been to see you I can say yes. And I'll still feel sub-human but she'll feel like a million bucks and she'll leave me alone.
But while I'm here, while I *choose* to be here, let me say this about that.
I don't know whether there's a God.
And I don't think you know either.
But you get paid to say there is and everybody's gotta make a living so that's fair ball.
But what I wanna know is how come I never see one of you guys come down to a picket line. Never once have I seen one of you people down on a picket line. Flood, fire and famine, yessiree bob, plane crashes, AIDS, war and pestilence, you guys show up in strength. But the second we call a strike, you call it quits. 18 *months* on a picket line, I see marriages busting up, kids gettin beat up at recess, sister hating sister, scabs eating our food, us lining up at the food bank, our kids wondering just what the hell is pissing all over their little parade. But the hot-line from God goes dead. Didn't my ex-wife need comfort? Didn't she need the comfort of words like "and the multitude was fed"? The multitude, you little limp turd, not just the shareholders, not just the the the, CEO. The *multitude.*
So what about it buddy? Is God really working for all of us?
Or is God just another *company* man?

Corruption.
Greed.
Murder.

You say these words to a journalist. I figure it's like heroin. Like a small pile of heroin on the coffee table. He ignores it for awhile. Then his feet start to sweat. He licks his lips. He gets out of the house, goes for a walk, goes for a drink, gets laid. He goes home. The heroin is still sitting there on his coffee table. He stalks around the house. He says: there's things I really should be getting on with. The Congo. Bosnia. Sri Lanka.
But it's heroin.
You say corruption greed and murder to a journalist.
He's thinking:
Government corruption.
Bagmen and payoffs.
A hit in a gravel pit, a bullet behind the ear.
He's thinking:
Just one little taste.
So my friend shows up. The journalist.
Still smelling like Paris.
He shows up at my kitchen door with a girl with a camera.
Looking for a taste.
We reminisce.
Yak yak yak.
Duty free scotch.
Yadda yadda yadda.
I tell him stories.
Drinking urine. The kobalds. The return of the sun.

I say:
Last week I'm watching the news. Some cop gets himself smoked over fifty bucks at a 7-11. A thousand cops show up at his funeral. Cubans from Florida, Mounties from Iqaluit. The widow's there, the kids, the preachers, the politicians howling about gun control and wrestling for the cameras. The flag. The national anthem. You know where my son showed up? He was a hiccup on the stocks page. Our stock went down a cent a share when they closed the shaft to dig his body out. Worth a penny a share for two days then he disappears from the papers for good. No parade. No picture

of him on the national news. They never pronounced his name wrong because they never said it at all.
But his name was: John Albert DeLormier.
John
Albert
DeLormier.

My friend asks me what I want.
I tell him it's simple.
I want my shift boss. I want the manager. I want the president, the CEO. I want everybody who ever made a dime on the company stock. I want the stock promoter and the secretary who types up the orders. And the little gray haired old lady who clips her coupons. I want them all.
I want justice.
I want revenge.
It's payback time.

My friend says:
I'm crying, Floyd. I'm weeping buckets. But it isn't news. It happens every day. You know who'd be interested in this story? Nobody. You know why? Read a book once in a while, you'd have read that a thousand times a million different ways. The business man who says: "Money has no heart conscience or homeland." The novelist who says: "the business of business — is murder." Politicians in the pockets of corporate mafioso? Blood on the balance sheet, profit equals death? I could write that. But I won't write that. It isn't news. Because, my friend, people like you don't even get newspaper boxes in your neighbourhoods anymore because you don't buy what the advertisers are selling. And if these guys don't give a shit if you *buy* their paper what makes you think they'll put you *in* it? You're waste circulation, my friend. Waste circulation. My friend. You don't exist.

He says this with loving kindness, words of wisdom to an idiot child. He is my friend.

My friend says: I do not exist.
My friend says: It isn't a story.
Do I throw him out?
I think about it.
Do I throw him out?
No. I need him.
He has skills.
He owns a laptop, he can type, he owns a fax machine, a Rolodex with the names of important people on it.
I need him to speak for me, to tell the story about the murder of intelligent worms, of whom my son is one, I need him to put it down in black and white, the blood on the balance sheet, so someone will pay.
I need him to tell the truth.
I need him.

Besides.
His girlfriend is beautiful.
And she skinny-dips in the river, she comes up from the river into the yard at dawn, dripping and beautiful, she stands in the kitchen dripping and beautiful and me insomniac at the kitchen table and stoned stupid and drooling, and she drips beautifully and I ask her if they are leaving:

And she says:
I'm doing a series of death masks: Women who sleep with convicted killers. War correspondents. That kind of thing. The living dead. I think you might be a good study: working eight hours a day, two hundred days a year a mile inside the earth, the ultimate graveyard shift. I want to see if I can see death in your eye. The bulge in your pants when the end comes close. Do you get that feeling? Nostalgia for oblivion? I think so. I think we all have a death wish. That's why we drive cars. The hole in the ozone is our doorway home.

And she takes my photograph.

She says:
The camera lies by omission: it removes the sound, smell, context. I can frame the shot to make the viewer feel sorry *for* you. But I prefer to draw you so the viewer gets the underbelly too. Profanity. Vulgarity. A little spray of piss-yellow green for your crotch. The blue of your collar, the red of your neck. The compensation cheques you drink. The bills your sister pays. I can draw those too. A few words splashed in the corner of my composition: "Fuck-stick." "Bitch." "Gimme gimme gimme." I can ruin your tragic little portrait with honesty. I can do that. I've been to art school.

Do I throw them out?
No.
I need him.
And she is beautiful. And she likes to be naked. And I like to watch her naked. And she likes to watch me watch.
Till I am lockjawed and crosseyed.
So I see a hooker.

You're gonna have to help me. Suggestions, ya know, I'll take suggestions. I'm not very, imaginative, when it comes to this stuff. I mean, I'm not a prude, I ain't too shy, but I don't think I have too much, imagination. When it comes to sex. Positions and stuff. Toys. Spanking, or whatever. Bondage. So now it's worse. The one thing I knew what to do with, however unimaginative, I have no use for. I have no use of.

A woman's hand, a woman's small hand, tuggin at my belt buckle. The taste of sweat. The way she curls her toes just before she comes . . . that little crack of the pelvic bone when she's tryna . . . that smile, that *smile* at the end.
Memory. God's gift to gimps.

So. What are we gonna do girl? Yeah. I can do that. I can do that too. I *like* to do that. Where were you when I was still human? OK. Let's get started.

And then I see a shrink.

Uh. I'm not quite sure if this is something for you or not. I mean, the physio girl's got me working on my plastic parts and the doctor wants to know where it hurts on the parts of me that are left but what I'm feeling is pain in a part of me that's buried in a dump someplace. I'm confused you see. Or maybe I'm not confused. Maybe what I am is pissed off. Maybe I want justice. Maybe instead of phantom pain in a leg that ain't working, maybe I want a phantom erection. Wouldn't that be justice? Couldn't do anything with it. But it might be a comfort to fall asleep with. Phantom hard-on, maybe even phantom wet dreams. How come there's no such thing as a phantom hard-on? That's what I'd call a psychological breakthrough. So whaddya think? Can you help me out?

Short answer? No.

And while I try to figure out how to convince my friend that I exist, I take him out on the river. And he drinks like a fish and he fishes like an American. And I'm not getting anywhere. So I talk some more to the girl with the camera. About my friend.

She says:
I get up in the morning. I shower. I wash off yesterday's grit. I wash yesterday off. One morning I tell him I was born to missionaries on a small island in the South China Sea. The next day I tell him that I was born in a one room trapper's shack to a woman with no teeth and no English. But it's all the same to him, whoever or whatever I was. He doesn't seem to remember. I think at first it's the alcohol: single malt amnesia. He quits drinking for awhile but the blackouts continue. Journalists are like that I suppose — no memory past yesterday. I get used to it. I get to like it. It makes for good sex. I'm anybody I want, the danger of the strange. New day. New story.

This doesn't help me.
I ask again.
She says:
I watch him. I like to watch him. I like to watch him mutate. I watch him working on a story about transients and I see him begin

to drift, become a drifter. I watch him work on a story about a lawyer and one night he'll come home with a new pair of shoes, a pair he can polish as shiny as a two dollar coin. When he writes the rodeo he walks bowlegged and spits out the window. When he writes Bay Street he's horny as a monkey and hard as a doorknob. Now he's here. The north. Muskeg and distance. Words he hasn't used in twenty years roll off his tongue. Snig. He wants to snig me in the back seat of the car. Moose hunting. Hockey. He talks in tongues. He mutates with geography. Depends who's paying.

She says:
You want something from him. So you have to give him something.
No whining — the age of the victim is over.
No begging.
Above all — no criticism: it's not that journalists are born thin-skinned. It's just that they're born without any skins at all.
No outrage.
No naiveté.
No good guy bad guy dialectic.
She says:
You can lock a woman in three different restaurants for sixty hours a week, and because it is three different restaurants, you can pay her minimum, no pension, no benefits, no protection. You can do that to her because her poverty is abstract. It doesn't really exist. You can take that woman's kid, send him to school with no breakfast, keep him too hungry to learn, and he's flunking out by grade six. You can do that to a kid — but you can't fuck him up the ass. If you put your penis in that little boy and get caught — that's news and you'll make the papers. You can send him to school hungry — his hunger doesn't exist. But touch his anus — and your dick is a headline.

She says:
Take a couple of totalitarian toads like Bill Gates and Conrad Black. A couple of power-mad little sadists for whom too much

power is almost enough. But their power isn't news. That is too abstract. But take another pair of sadistic toads like Karla Homulka and Paul Bernardo, a lovely little tag-team who like to tie up children and fuck them after they are dead. Take a couple of sexual terrorists for whom the only kick is also power — now that is a saleable product.

She says:
You wanna be news?
You gotta be sexy.
You wanna be sexy?
You gotta have an angle.
You wanna have an angle?
You gotta take a risk.
She says: you have a secret. I see it in the photographs I take of you. The camera sucks the secret out of your guts and deposits it on the negative for everyone to see.
She says: take a knife from the kitchen, sharpen this knife with stone and spit, pour yourself a double shot and split your belly from button to breastbone. Now reach up and in and haul out that beating secret and dump it on the kitchen table
a little bleeding dwarf.
She says:
you think this is the age of the microchip and the 500 channel universe and knowledge at the speed of light. Nice try. This is still the age of dirt. Lucrative, potent, tactical — dirt.

You have one card to play. Your dirty little secret. Lay it on the table — your dirty little dwarf, all blood and noise. Go ahead.
And she takes a photograph.
Death mask.

I have secrets. That I steal more than I earn and beg more than I steal. Lies, bad debts and poaching in the park and lying to income tax, the car I steal from myself to claim insurance. Knocking on a back door cause my buddy's pulling a double shift and his young wife alone damp with anticipation.

Just second-string guilt.
So up the ante.
Check and call.

I tell her a story. But fuck her, she's been to art school, she's gonna have to read between the lines.
I tell her:
The day in question is no different than any other day.
You shave an hour off your time which means extra production. Extra production means extra profit. Extra profit means extra dividends. Extra dividends means bonuses all down the trickle-down line.
Doctor cuts a patient's visit short, squeezes in two more by the end of the day. Trucker running overweight and overspeed. Lawyer skips pages fifty through ninety on a finding. Contractor gives you twenty year shingles for your roof when you paid for thirty. Don't even look over your shoulder. Everybody knows. Shift boss says, manager says, president says, shareholders say.
I tell my son: payday's Friday.
Day in question is no different than any other day.
Standard operating procedure.
Business as usual.

She's good at reading between the lines.
She says:
Not bad. Not bad at all.

So I tell my friend.
Word by word.
Every machine we didn't take the time to maintain. Every bit of fuel stored within easy reach and against the regs.
I tell him: blood on the paycheques.
I tell him drop by drop.
He says, well, he says, coy as a part-time virgin. That might be news.

The newspaper comes out Wednesday morning. Wednesday afternoon my son's wife — my son's young widow — is pounding on my kitchen door.

She says:
Bastard.
She says:
Fucking bastard.
She says:
Killer.
She says:
Your son.
She says:
My lover.
She says, her wedding ring digging into my eyeball:

scab.

I close the door.

An investigation.

I don't wanna answer those questions. Here's the only answer you're gonna get — I'm a gimp. Clear? And the widows, asshole, isn't that answer enough? You think you got questions, no, I got questions, and if I thought you two had a brain between you I'd ask em. But you don't so I won't so get the fuck out of here before I momentarily forget the high regard in which I hold the law enforcement personnel of this good and great democracy. Because I would hate to do that, forget the good job you do in protecting my place of employment from scabs. I would hate to forget that before the blind eyes of justice everyone on the picket line, both the employer and the employee, are exact equals. You see, I am capable of doubting such self-evident truths, I confess to momentary bouts of suspicion, so I give you fair warning: Get the fuck out you toads, you company men, you hole lickers, get out you scabs.

I close the door.

An arrest.

But what if I want to talk? What if I want to tell you what's on my mind? Here's a thought: I think pigs is a good name for you two. You live in this town, you work in this town, you raise your kids in this town. But what you really do in this town is shit where you eat. You weren't born here, you're not gonna die here, you're just putting in two years with isolation pay and then you're gone. But I — I gotta walk in pig shit from the outskirts to mainstreet, your pig shit, your duty, just doing your *duty*, your job, arrest a man, the wrong man, an innocent man, because the dollar talks and pigs have ears.
Now cuff me.
Or I'll shove that pepper spray right up your ass.

Someone opens a door for me.
A cell.

I read the papers. Watch the news. I'm looking to see who's going down with me. Water pouring in between the ribs, my feet getting wet, ankles getting wet, life jackets starting to float, up to my ass, water spilling in over the gunnels.

There's lots of room in this canoe.
But I'm going down solo.
Everybody else waving from the portage.
Looks like a lovely shore lunch.

Surprise, surpise, surprise.

What did I expect?

Every morning I get up. I drink my coffee, I eat my bacon and eggs. I get in a wire cage that drops me fourteen hundred feet straight down. I expect the cable to hold, the brakes to work. And if the cable don't hold or the brakes don't brake or if the cageman is drunk or having a heart attack, I expect the dogs to stop that cage before it hits the bottom at two hundred miles an hour and driving my heels through my eye sockets on impact.
I expect things to work.

I expect there to be air at the bottom of the shaft, pumped thousands of feet straight down by machines machined and welded by men and women working by the hour and subject to human frailty and hangovers and divorce and plain old inattention but I expect those machines to pump me air.
I expect the roof bolts to hold and the timbers not suddenly to turn into plastecine.
I expect the rules of physics and geology not to change overnight, even if those rules and laws of physics and geology are just the theorizing of men and women with laptops and degrees.
I expect things to work.
Because if I didn't expect things to work, there is no way in hell I would get in a cage that drops me into the centre of the earth five days a week at 1570 feet per minute.
Because if things don't work . . .

I say this to my friend.
He shrugs he smiles he says:
white wine or red
salad or steak
boys or girls —
you choose.
Short cuts in the belly of the earth
or living by a code
a nearly free man in a nearly free country
short cuts in the belly of the beast
yes or no —
you choose.

And the girl with the camera says:
you wanna be news you gotta be sexy you wanna be sexy you gotta have an angle you wanna have an angle you gotta take a risk you wanna take a risk —
your call.

I say to my friend:
So is the plan working? That's all I want to know. Is the plan.

Working. Cause I don't work. My leg doesn't work. My pecker's on permanent disability. No money. No friends. No family. And the cops have made up my bunk at the Plexiglass Hotel. So tell me. Is the plan. Working.

He says:
I'm a story teller. That's what I do. That's *all* I do. I follow the beast where it leads. I track it down and I nail it. I'm not responsible for its actions — I record its actions. The beast is free to act — I'm obligated to record. That's it, that's all. I'm a story*teller.* Don't look at me like that. Don't *look* at me like that. What do I do? What do I *do*? I listen. I write. Period. That's what I do. I listen. I write. I'm just the secretary, OK? All I do is send the memos from this toilet. That should be the name of your story: Memos From a Toilet. You wanted me here. You *wanted* me to do what I do. Right? *Right?* Right.

I'm thinking:
No.
I'm saying:
Once upon a time there was a little boy who watched a black and white TV. He lay on his belly on the cool wooden floor nose to the screen with *Hockey Night in Canada.* One night he stays up late, his parents drinking in the kitchen. He watches the 11 o'clock news. There is a man with a microphone standing in a field in a faraway country. There are soldiers. There is gunfire. The man with the microphone is telling a story, and even though he does not understand it, it is the most interesting story the little boy has ever heard. And he forgets about the railroad or flying twin Otters and even forgets about the NHL. And he decides right there, his parents screaming in the kitchen, the wooden floor cool on his belly, that he will grow up to tell stories on the 11 o'clock news. And when the little boy grows up he goes to school and there he learns a phrase that warms his little Christian heart: "To afflict the comfortable, to comfort the afflicted."
But something happens.
The little boy is older. His name is known and his bank account

is healthy. And the words that warmed his little Christian heart have shifted and changed. And he kicks the afflicted. And he licks the comfortable.

He shrugs again, he smiles again, he says:
Buy a dictionary. Look up the word — power.
And then he disappears. Telling sexy stories. His girlfriend taking pictures.

Court is quick and dirty. I plead stupid. I plead sorry. I plead making a living.
And the judge gives me five years cause that's how he makes his living.

Five years.
Breakfast dinner supper
breakfast dinner supper
breakfast dinner supper.
Just like detox. One day at a time.

I learn some new songs. The Stones
Sister Morphine.

A con falls in love with me.
But that's another story.

I do three years.
I get a parole hearing.
I tell the board about sleepless nights. And no appetite. And my son's broken face in the mirror when I shave. I tell them about eyes that don't see and fingers that don't clench. I tell them about widows.
And because they don't read between the lines I tell them about greed and stupidity and blindness and sin. And I tell them about crime and criminality and I tell them about venality cause I buy a dictionary and I been studying words and they still aren't reading between the lines so I tell them about thuggery and duplicity and treachery and fraud and deception. And I'm really getting rolling

now and they're digging it and digging me and I'm telling them about savages and bullies and barbarians and mercenaries and crimes against humanity and the slaughter of the innocents. And they're creaming their jeans these parole board appointees at sixty five thousand a year cause its who you know to blow. I'm telling them this story about murder and destruction and ruin and waste and eradication and extermination.
And pain. And torture. And death.
And because the good citizens can't read between the lines
they think I'm talking about
me.
And they sign my release.
And they call me free.

Except that isn't what happens at all.
It's what I planned to say.
The little storyteller's trick I intended to pull.
I wanted them to wake up one night and finally read between the lines, wake up one night and see that they were right there in the cast of characters, *dramatis personae*, antagonist and protagonist, blood under the nails.
But that isn't the story.

I listen to a lot of stories in jail.
I hear a lot of things:
I'm gonna get that guy
Just wait'll I get out
his fault
her fault
somebody's fault
the school
the judge
the boss
the lawyer
the politician.
Them.
Them.

Them.
Them.
I hear a lot of stories in jail. All of them the same one.

I buy a dictionary. I look up *power.*
I buy a dictionary of clichés and I look up:
that's the way it is.
I buy all kinds of dictionaries and I look up *idealism* and *childish* and *wishful thinking* and *realpolitik* and *real world* and *grow up* and *what did you expect* and *money talks. Dog eat dog. Buy low sell high.* I buy a dictionary and I look up *if I don't do it somebody else will.*
I buy a dictionary and I look up *cynical.*
I buy a dictionary and I look up — *collusion.* I didn't know how to spell collusion, one *l* or two, but I find it. And I find *consent.* And *collaboration.* And all those 10 dollar words for stupid.

I hear a lot of talk in jail. I remember a lot, too.
Hospital trains in Sudbury yard. Stock trains to the slaughter-house. A screaming girl on a skidoo.

And so I tell the parole board about the ice.

I tell them about my dad leaving camp in the morning, grocery list poking out of his work shirt pocket. Me and my older sister are struggling with the weight of the gas cans, the cedar strip boat red as a new caboose, the engine a Johnson Seahorse, older than I am right now, bigger than I was back then.

My dad clambers to the back of the boat and we nudge him off the shore, the engine catching on the second crank. The boat whips round he waves again, the sound shrinking into silence around the point.

Then in for a swim, a load of kindling into grampa's camp or wrestling with the dog — but watching every boat on the river, waiting for our family sound.

Late in the afternoon a red boat cuts round the point, sounds right yes looks right yes one guy yes — but no, it swings too far east and I droop a bit — but maybe he's coming a different way around the weed-bed — but maybe it isn't even him. Then he's close to shore and he's grinning cause he's fooled me again and the dog sprints barking along the beach, the waves washing up behind the boat, the smell of gas and exhaust, a hug from my father his breath sweet from a quick beer snatched in the Legion in an asphalt noon I didn't have to know.

Then the groceries, meat and butter and watch that bag its got the eggs and apples and pop and rum for the folks, newspapers coal-oil mail and a hint of small-town news for my mother. And little sister blonde hair flagging in the breeze her arms wrapped tight around a cool green watermelon half her weight.

Then the ice.

Cut from the winter river by rough young men who laughed as they worked, tonging the huge blocks into the iron boxes slung under the passenger trains, the ice wagon groaning on the station platform.

But the ice is ours now, the too-small pieces slipped from the ice house, chunks of ice and sawdust and burlap and my father huffing them up the hill one two three and a sack for grandpa too.

And my job, my job is chipping the chunks into the icebox with a screwdriver, the bacon, burger, the chops stuffed in around. And chipping the ice I'm dreaming. I'm dreaming of my own triumphant return home, home with the goodies, the supplies, that cowboy word, that hero's word, supplies. And I'm puffing them up the hill, the fifty pound sacks, huffing them up the hill for my own son to chip, the cold meltwater soaking my shirt.

And I'm working like a father in the sun-burn heat.
And that's all I ever want to do.
Work like a father in the sun-burn heat.

But grampa dies.
And the red boat burns.

And then I kill my kid for coins in a piggy bank.
And that's the story:
Beginning.
Middle.
And end.

Coins.

That's what I tell the parole board.
And they sign my release.
They let me out.
They call me free.

My friend sends me a postcard and a stack of newspapers. Jerusalem. London. Ottawa. I don't see you in here, he says. Do you?

Everything I know begins and ends around a kitchen table. A funeral. A new baby born. A new job. A marriage gone ripe. Any decision or change at all. It all begins right here. Over coffee. Over beer. Over over-proof Jamaican rum, you talk it over right here.
Whatever happens, a skidoo through the ice, your kid's first pickerel, you bring it all back here and you lay it out between the ashtrays and the needles and you tell it. Again and again. Right here between the bottles and the knives.
Where you bury your own dead
until your arms go numb.
Where you tell your own story
until your gums bleed black.

He says: I don't exist.
He says: This isn't a story.

But this is the end.
Or the beginning.

Your call.

Lucy B. says:

In a rented room above the Lochalsh store
I spread these rented knees.

Northern lights waltz
green dawn behind the curtain.

Sunday: rinse my mouth with rye
scrub a black sheet gray.

Sun-up stalled today behind the hill.
They warned me that might happen.

A baggageman knits my throat with new red ribbon.
And then he lays me out.

Four Eyes says:

He loved comic books and nothing else
Superman and Spidy
Sargeant Rock, the Blackhawks.

We called him Scramble, something to do
with revolving fathers, the spare-board brakemen
who bunked with his mom then switched out.
Scrambled I guess but Jesus
what a rack of comics
a small-fry fortune in pulp and ink
driving hard deals down the basement on Saturday afternoons.

Scramble traded with me a few miles down the track
would one-hand himself like Superboy onto the side of a boxcar

taxi down the line, his red scarf flagging
hop off bang in front of my house
haggle till suppertime.

One day in March he grabs a stock-train
cows pissing through the slats.
Crazy Scramble
he knows the stock-trains highball to the slaughterhouse.
Crazy Scramble thinks he's Superman.

The stock-train picking up speed
Scramble's fingers going slack
doing thirty when he smears the switch stand.
A quick flock of heroes papers the air.
Superboy's cape flaps into the snow.

Aunt Bev says:

Most nights I'd sleep right through his call
just hear him puttering in the kitchen, packing his grip.
I'd get up, the tea well steeped, the kitchen warm.
We'd talk for an hour or so
the town snoring. Some women I know, their husbands get up
get up and go, go bull with the boys in the Yard Office.
He taught me euchre one night, waiting for his train.
So we'd sit and talk, then he'd go off
I'd check the kids and roll back into sleep.

But if he was out on the road and a call would
come at three a.m. or four I'd jump at the first ring
my heart kicking the doors of my ribs.
But it would be a wrong number
or my damn fool brother on a tear
and I'd be standing in the cold hallway
some mute thing climbing onto me.

Well.

I unplug the phone at night now, too late I know.
But I still have the kids, all working in the south.
And when the next news comes I want to be up and
on my feet.

Dougie D says:

My aunt was a good old girl with a joke up her sleeve, lean over the fence to take or tell the news, arrange flowers at a funeral, go dancing at the Legion on Friday night. She ran the hockey pool for forty years, hated every ref for two hundred miles. Saturday nights if Detroit was on TV she stayed home to watch. Otherwise she'd pack a 26er in her purse and head for the rink. When I was learning to walk she bought me a hockey stick for balance. When the other boys were out on the road trying to stickhandle around their old man, my aunt was teaching me the moves that made Gordie Howe Gordie Howe. I made all-star my first season.

Once upon a time the weekends were fairy tales, and if you played Junior B. you were a knight, armour and all. It was better than drugs or rock n roll. End to end rushes, the Roman howl from the wooden bleachers, old women whose sons had grown up to be only accountants laughing and cheering like hell. Then trooping soaking wet through the cold air to the steam-heated dressing rooms. Small boys begging for the cracked stick, like what, a talisman, the skill of the stick to be passed on in ceremony. Something like that maybe.

In the dressing room the memories to come would be back-slapped into life like babies: "I drop my shoulder and the defence goes left, I'm going right, there's the goddamn net big as a duck-blind, goalie's all goggle-eyed, I deke him dickless, the red light flares and we're one up and not looking back . . . "

New York has Broadway. We had the boardway. A few years piling 2x4s you get your big break and move into the mill — big chance to lose a mitt, an eye, your hearing. I know one guy . . . You might have read in the paper about how he tipped in. Debarker. Pretty sensational. Had to be. Hard to make the papers living north of Barrie. Buried his steel-toes.

The first chance I got — gone. I wasn't going to be sitting there, afraid to go, nothing changing but the breakfast special going up a dime at a time, the only ticking of the clock, ten cents a year.

But those frozen weekend nights. The owner of the bar buying a round for the team every time we won and we won a lot. Oh yeah, we drank for free for a time. I pay for my own beer belly now, but yeah, once upon a time . . .

A tall Finn girl with a smile like milk and money. I can see her up in the stands, a halo of warm breath, I can hear that one soft voice rise in a whisper above the noise of the crowd. She used to pick me up after practice and we'd walk the streets, the sky flashing green. We used up all the words in two languages and we still couldn't say what it was we wanted, dreaming under that cold green sky. I don't miss all that. I don't even think I miss her. I just wonder where she is, who she is and how she got there. But I remember warming my fingers on her belly, her breath in my mouth, and no matter what she drank she always tasted of tangerines.

Flying, yeah. I flew until I was 18, never landed once. I believed everything everybody said about me, I was crown prince, going to the top. I lasted two days at a Junior A tryout, never got my stick on the puck in scrimmage, never saw the hits coming. Shifts lasted a thousand years, puking between my blades after every one.

I don't mind this journeyman life after the long tease. But it was a tease. Hell, I was playing old-timer when I was 20 years old.

Mickey says:

Crip. Stump. Hook.
Every freight train gimped
the tail-end crew just gangrene
a stump of box-car where my old job rode.

> We're fishing off the trestle at Poulin.
> His plastic hand falls into the creek

my uncle burps gin.
Grab a hold of yourself, gurgles his wife my aunt
grab a hold of yourself. They laugh, I, ten,
peek up his empty sleeve
my intestines torquing.

Accountants flash scalpels
the bone-saw grunts.
Black ink, phantom
pain.

Kenny R. says:

Talking books in the tavern he drinks and smirks yeah
he says yeah, a novel so Canadian
it even had a scene on a train.

The foreign still in vogue (forever and amen)
Virginia Woolf and Oscar
or even Jesse James. Crack house out in St. Henri?
Leather bars? L.A.? Yes
keep it urban just keep that edge.
Like steam and steel and diesel
small towns tut tut
cliché.
Done and done to
death.

Done to death. Agreed:

~~Dalton~~.
~~Kormac~~.
~~Island Lake~~.
~~Lochalsh.~~

Sam Jr. says:

Ghost trains
Ghost towns
Ghost travellers

Some nights when the telephone rings
its only our dead on the end of the line.

Some nights when the telephone rings
a dead man takes the call.

On the edge of his chair on the outskirts of the night
a conductor waits for his train
his eyes signal-red he's been waiting for years
hand shakin pouring the tea
the telephone rings —
he checks his kids he kisses his wife he's out the door
he's walking in the cool night air
his father's father's watch tickin honest in his pocket
his house his town his world
snoring safe and the diesels rumbling just as safe just up the street

The telephone rings on the outskirts of the night
it rings it rings it rings
so the call-boy goes hunting down the tail-end brakeman
cruises town on a CCM with busted light and a banana seat
he checks the pool room the taproom the girlfriend's room
he checks the Legion Hall and the restaurant
finds Sonny down behind the high school
playin scrub with a day-glo softball
northern lights washin green over God's lazy face
callboy calls you gotta call Sonny you finally got a call
and Sonny at the plate whacks high and inside out to the river
the day-glo ball bobs like a lifeboat in the slow black water
got a call Sonny grins
gonna pay gotta pay wanta pay my bills

The telephone rings on the outskirts of the night
a hard-drinkin hog-head namea Oily takes her on the first ring
takes his first call in thirty years stumbles to the fridge
with a rot gut ache
he packs his grip grinnin
he's called for a highball headdin east lickety split
lickety split the clickety clack of a highball rollin east

The clickety clack of the telegraph too
though the wire's been sold off for scrap
the clickety clack the yakety yak
the yard office simply ahum ahum ahum
you hear us all again we've all taken the call
firemen signalmen baggagemen
a world of men farting and swearing talking track-speed and women
operators roadmasters car knockers the boss the brass
we've all taken the call
the first call in years
and you say to Jimmy hey Jimmy how's it goin
can't kick says Jimmy who retired in forty
can't kick he says Jesus Christ I can barely walk
but he's down here tonight he misses the boys he misses railroadin
it gets in your blood though your blood burns dirty as coal.

The telephone wakes us at the edge of our dreams
goin trappin goin fishin goin shoppin in the city
second year of college five years on the job
goin east goin west
and the long long gone comin home for the funerals —
auntie uncle grampa best friend —
we're all comin and goin and the waiting room fills
and that train pulls in and we're rollin
now we're rollin

Thirty miles out from the edge of the end
a trackman's house and the kitchen lights on
you know this fellow, his kids and his wife

cause 20 years gone on a no-moon night
Bust a boxcar knuckle and the snow waist deep
not his job at all but he's workin on his knees
the lady's pourin coffee at forty two below
yeah you know these people
yeah you know this road
now you're rollin
you're rollin

The telephone rings now she's rollin
steel biting into steel rollin rollin
it's hard to talk its hard to walk
the radio has a stutter
but the dispatchers givin you clear after clear after clear
you never take the hole you never get scooped
the track bed's a cloud
you're flying like god
you got fast orders
you're rollin
you're rollin

In the heart of the heart of the bush now
you're rollin
rollin towards the sun
mist on the river
bull moose in the swamp
you're rollin
you whistle for the crossing a loon calling back
loon cry and whistle whistle and loon cry
the steel singin ahead of the wheels
she's rollin
steel singin
loon callin
you're rollin
a wolf on the treeline
a wolf rare as money
you're rollin

rollin
east to the sun

The telephone rings you're sixteen and wild
and a rock n roll show comes to town not your town
Maple Leaf Gardens is twelve hours east on short steel and slag
and 902 sits quivering at the fuel stand
You crawl into the second unit
some old guy bummin from the west lying dirty on the floor
rollin through Sudbury yards and the railroad cops
rollin into West Toronto
old guy steppin off the runnin board
his ankles too old his toes too slow
boy how he bounces bouncity bouncity bounce bounce in the Parkdale slag
but you come off grinnin just sixteen years of piss and vinegar
and steppin into rollin space
you hit the slag steamin

you're dreamin
the Gardens ahowl with a rock n roll band
a brown-eyed girl dancing pretty in her seat
those nipples dancing in a tie-dyed shirt
she dances
you're rollin
she dances
you're dreamin
she dances
she dances

You're twelve years tall rollin west from Montreal
mom and dad whisper weird and low
"the end of the money" and the "what we gonna do?"
cause it's years before plastic
credit cards still just a wet dream in some banker's sheets
but Jesus Christ must be ridin this coach
cause your father's last dollar brings five plates of grub

the waiter just railroadin, takin care of his own
and the night rolls you sleepy
rolls you dreamless on the steel
rollin
rollin
rollin you home

You're six years old nose flat to the glass
you're rollin
tradin black spruce swamp for fields full of cities
a spankin new world for your little bright eyes
happy birthday-merry christmas all rolling into one
living the changes
not arrival or departure
this journey's a gift they'll never take away
the newsie in the aisle selling chocolate milk n'magazines
the planet big n' swellin bigger with the Indian names:
Nemegosenda. Biscotasing. Pogamasing.
You're rollin you're rollin
not Arrivals or Depature lounge
but the real of the rollin
the words and the faces and the stories
the living
and the dying
and the dead
she's rollin
she's rollin
she's rollin

and the great north land gives a shiver when the ghost trains
run

and the great shield quivers when the ghosts trains
roll.

She says:

An east-bound freight drinks at the fuel stand
he shivers with the crows
hopping foot to foot for warmth.
Clear signal, second hoot of the whistle, the tonnage groans.
He swings up on and in, crouches
in the rolling dark of the second unit
eyes the door for the railroad cop. Safe.
He spins a thermos cap, tea with lemon
sipping at warmth, mainlining stars.
In the fireman's seat he dreams
I dance dipped in white icing up the aisle
wet dreams of me and him and me and wakes
at dawn in the black INCO hills of Sudbury
to buy these diamond slivers.

Printed in November 1997 by

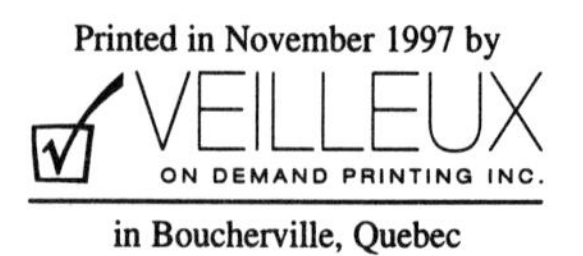

in Boucherville, Quebec